To my friend Carol, for comics and social justice.
– David

For my children, Jacob and Luna;
my art is a love song to you both.
– Steve

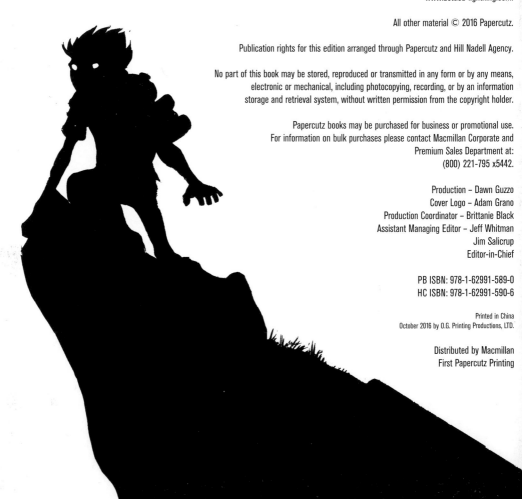

THE ONLY LIVING BOY #3 "Once Upon a Time"

Chapters 5 and 6:
Writer/ Co-Creator: David Gallaher
Artist/ Co-Creator: Steve Ellis
Color Flatting: Holley McKend
Lettering: Melanie Ujomori
Consulting Editor: Janelle Asselin
Assistants: Emily Walton, Arycal Jackson

Originally serialized at: www.the-only-living-boy.com

Papercutz books may be purchased for business or promotional use.
For information on bulk purchases please contact Macmillan Corporate and
Premium Sales Department at:
(800) 221-795 x5442.

Production – Dawn Guzzo
Cover Logo – Adam Grano
Production Coordinator – Brittanie Black
Assistant Managing Editor – Jeff Whitman
Jim Salicrup
Editor-in-Chief

PB ISBN: 978-1-62991-589-0
HC ISBN: 978-1-62991-590-6

Printed in China
October 2016 by O.G. Printing Productions, LTD.

Distributed by Macmillan
First Papercutz Printing

CHAPTER FIVE

Previously in...

THE ONLY LIVING BOY

Twelve-year-old Erik Farrell continues his journey through a patchwork planet. After escaping the Groundling's city, Erik and his lucky medallion reunite with his friends Morgan and Thea. He convinces the Mermidonians to allow Thea to leave, even though her impending "Chrysalis" could threaten them all. Dodging monsters along the way, the friends make their way to Thea's flying city, Sectuarius. Thea's mother, the queen, says she can help restore Erik's memories. But just as he begins to see glimpses of the life he led, Doctor Once's minions attack and Erik and his friends must defend the Chrysalis chamber from his experiments. Erik fights hard, but soon he's falling through the clouds, until he wakes up in a place both familiar and alien...and finds his mother! Is Erik truly home?

DON'T YOU WISH YOU COULD JUST START OVER...

WIPE AWAY ALL OF THE MISTAKES?

BUT, IT DOESN'T WORK THAT WAY.

I REALLY NEED YOU TO BE ON YOUR BEST BEHAVIOR, ERIK.

REMEMBER... "WHEN THINGS DON'T GO ACCORDING TO PLAN..."

"ROLL WITH IT," I KNOW.

THAT'S RIGHT. NO MORE STUNTS. FACE THIS CHALLENGE LIKE A MAN.

But I'm not a man, I'm a boy.

NEW YORK

WHEN YOU'RE DONE, HELP ME IN THE LIVING ROOM.

RUNNING AWAY?

THAT WOULD BE THE EASY THING TO DO.

FACING THE SHAME...

...THAT'S MUCH HARDER.

HIDING FROM YOUR MISTAKES ONLY MAKES YOU WEAK.

I KNOW THAT NOW.

LIVING ROOM

ASK YOURSELF THIS QUESTION:

WHAT IS THE DUMBEST POSSIBLE THING YOU COULD EVER DO?

AND HOW DO YOU LIVE WITH YOURSELF KNOWING IT CAN'T BE UNDONE?

I THINK YOU'RE GOING TO HAVE A REALLY SUCCESSFUL DAY TODAY, ERIK.

YOUR SCHOOL IS PERFECT FOR NON-TRADITIONAL LEARNERS.

DREAMS

IT'S NOT LIKE YOUR OLD SCHOOL AT ALL.

BUT I LOVED MY OLD...

SCHOOL!

METS
Acceptance Letter

POLICE LINE DO NOT CROSS

POLICE LINE DO NOT C

WAIT...

It didn't happen like that, did it?

MOM...

WHAT IS IT, SWEETIE?

WHAT EXACTLY ARE WE DOING HERE?

WHAT DO YOU MEAN?

I MEAN, ARE WE PACKING OR ARE WE UNPACKING?

WE'RE UNPACKING WHAT WE NEED AND PACKING UP THE REST.

BUT...MOM... THERE ARE SOME THINGS WE SHOULDN'T PACK AWAY.

OH, ERIK.

WE'VE BEEN OVER THIS.

A NEW HOME IS A WONDERFUL PLACE TO UNPACK OLD MEMORIES AND MAKE NEW ONES.

THERE'S SO MUCH STUFF THAT YOU'VE ACCUMULATED...

...IT'S HARD TO FIND QUITE WHAT WE'RE LOOKING FOR.

KITCHEN

BUT... I WANT TO TALK ABOUT THIS. WE NEVER TALK ABOUT THIS.

Daily Sta

METS STUDENT KILLED IN CAR CRASH

NOW IS NOT THE TIME, ERIK.

FAMILY STUFF

PLEASE, THIS WILL GO MUCH EASIER IF YOU WOULD JUST COOPERATE.

THAT GIVES ME AN IDEA.

YOU TOLD ME THAT I HAVE TO FIGHT FOR WHAT I BELIEVE IN.

SO I'M GOING TO FOLLOW YOUR LEAD. AND I'M GOING TO FIGHT UNTIL EVERY CAGE IS EMPTY.

GUARDS!

GUARDS!

SOME DAYS, YOUR BAD DECISIONS WILL STARE YOU RIGHT IN THE FACE.

WHAT IS IT, WHELP?

BUT THAT'S WHEN YOU STARE RIGHT BACK AT THEM WITH A SMILE.

BRING ME TO DOCTOR ONCE! I'LL TELL HIM EVERYTHING I KNOW.

YOU HAVE TO BE BRAVE.

NOW WE'VE GOT YOU ALL CLEANED UP, AND OUT OF THAT SOILED CLOTHING.

JUST LIKE THE DOCTOR ORDERED.

EVEN WHEN YOU DON'T WANT TO BE.

SO GET IN THERE!

YOU HAVE TO HAVE COURAGE.

THE COURAGE TO KNOW THAT YOU'RE DOING THE RIGHT THING.

YOU HAVE TO HAVE HOPE.

BEAR!

EVEN WHEN OTHERS TRY TO TAKE IT FROM YOU.

YES... YOUR TRUSTED COMPANION...

AND NOW, MY LITTLE... HOSTAGE...

I SAID I'D TELL YOU WHAT I KNOW...

I SAW HOW YOU USED THIS THING TO ORCHESTRATE YOUR ESCAPE FROM THE CENSUS.

YOU WERE BLUFFING THEN.

YOU ARE BLUFFING NOW.

Leave Bear alone.

WHAT SORT OF GAME ARE YOU PLAYING, BOY?

YOUR FAILURE IS INEVITABLE.

YOU HAVE TO KEEP FIGHTING.

ENOUGH!

CRASH

AS I SAID, BOY... YOU'RE MERELY AN ANNOYANCE.

EVEN WHEN THE BAD GUYS WIN...

I TRIED TO DO THIS THE GENTLE WAY.

BUT YOU'VE LEFT ME WITH NO OTHER OPTIONS.

YOU HAVE TO KEEP FIGHTING.

THIS MACHINE IS MORE INVASIVE THAN THE LAST, IT WILL TELL ME EVERYTHING I NEED TO KNOW ABOUT YOU.

YOU CAN NEVER STOP FIGHTING.

YOU NEVER KNOW WHO IS DEPENDING ON YOU.

CHAPTER SIX

I HAVE TO BELIEVE THAT I CAN'T BE BROKEN.

IT IS MY MOST DANGEROUS OF MACHINES-- THE ASSEMBLER.

EVEN IF I AM.

IT WILL SCAN AND RESTORE YOUR SHATTERED MEMORIES.

YOU CAN'T DO THIS!

TAKING WHAT IS BROKEN AND GIVING IT NEW LIFE IS WHAT I DO.

IN THE PROCESS, ALL OF YOUR DARKEST SECRETS WILL BE REVEALED.

PLEASE TRY TO STAY STILL.

THE SIDE-EFFECTS MAY BE UNPLEASANT.

CLICK

41

FOR DECADES, MY MACHINES WOULD FAIL TO FULFILL THEIR TRUE POTENTIAL.

BUT WHAT KIND OF SCIENTIST WOULD I BE IF I JUST GAVE UP?

Stop it...

NOW... WHERE DID I PUT THE MIND MATRIX?

MY TECHNOLOGY WAS BORN FROM HUNDREDS OF FAILURES.

YOU KNOW WHAT FAILURE IS LIKE, DON'T YOU, BOY?

AH...YES. HERE IT IS!

WHILE THE ASSEMBLER REPAIRS YOUR BROKEN MEMORIES...

...THIS HELMET LETS ME TO STEP INTO YOUR MIND AND EXPERIENCE YOUR LIFE FIRSTHAND.

AFTER ALL, WHAT IS SCIENCE WITH-OUT MEANINGFUL OBSERVATION?

NOW...

YOU'VE KEPT THE WHOLE CLASS WAITING FOR YOU.

I'm sorry. I didn't mean to.

I THOUGHT YOU WERE SUPPOSED TO BE GIFTED?

HOW DID THEY LET YOU BACK IN?

WHAT WERE YOU THINKING?

WHY DID YOU EVEN BOTHER?

I KNOW WE'RE RUNNING VERY LATE, STUDENTS...

...BUT WE'LL MAKE SURE YOU ALL GET TO WHERE YOU NEED TO GO.

YOU MADE ME LATE FOR SOCCER PRACTICE, JERK!

HEY, SPACE CADET, I'M TALKING TO YOU!

45

I KNOW QUITE A BIT ABOUT GRAVITY AND YOU SEEM TO KNOW A COUPLE OF THINGS ABOUT SCIENCE AND STUFF.

SURE, I'M PRETTY GOOD AT SCIENCE AND STUFF.

SO YES?

YES.

THESE LIGHTS, HUH?

YEAH, THEY TAKE FOREVER.

AND THEN THEY CHANGE SO QUICK.

YOU ALMOST HAVE TO RUN TO OUTRACE THEM.

WANNA RACE?

YOU BET.

RUN!

WALK

I'M...

GONNA...

DONT WALK

COME ON, SLOWPOKE! WHAT ARE YOU WAITING FOR? HURRY UP!

HOOOOONK!

CATCH...

DONT WALK

...YOU.

IMPOSSIBLE. THIS SYNCHRONICITY CANNOT EXIST...

AND YET, WITH AN INFINITE NUMBER OF REALITIES, THE IMPOSSIBLE BECOMES POSSIBLE.

THINK OF ALL OF THE QUANTUM PROCESSES THAT MUST HAVE OCCURRED TO BRING US TO THIS MOMENT.

IT WAS, PERHAPS, INEVITABLE THE TEMPORAL ENERGIES IN THIS CREATURE WOULD BRING YOU TO ME.

I HAD FORGOTTEN HOW MUCH SHE LOVED YOU.

I WAS ASKED TO BUILD A NEW WORLD--A WORLD UNLIKE ANY OTHER.

A TWISTED WORLD THAT REFLECTED BAALIKAR'S OWN DARK SELF IMAGE.

I SCANNED ENDLESS UNIVERSES TO FIND WORLDS THAT WOULD BE PERFECT FOR THE PILLAGING.

MY HOME WAS TO BE MY FIRST TARGET.

IN THAT MOMENT, I FOUND SOMETHING TO FIGHT FOR.

I FOUND SOMETHING TO LIVE FOR.

I PLANNED OUR ESCAPE, JUST ME AND ZEE.

I RETRIEVED HER ESSENCE FROM THE CONSORTIUM...

...AND TUCKED HER AWAY SOME-PLACE SPECIAL.

THERE'S A BREACH IN THE FACILITY, DOCTOR!

LOOK'S LIKE IT'S US AGAINST THE WORLD, BEAR!

EEEOOOOo

EEEOOOOo

WE NEED TO GET YOU TO SAFETY!

OKAY... SO WE HAVE TO MOVE FAST, FELLA.

BUT...

BREAK THE DOOR DOWN!

EEEOOOOo

NOT WITHOUT THIS.

EEEOOOOo

EEEOOOOo

LIFE IS TOUGH.

EEEO OOO

TERRIBLE THINGS WILL HAPPEN.

YOU WILL NOT DESERVE THEM.

YOU WILL WANT TO ESCAPE FROM THEM.

WATCH OUT FOR PAPERCUTZ™

Welcome to the tangled and twisted third THE ONLY LIVING BOY graphic novel, by David Gallaher and Steve Ellis, from Papercutz–those comicbook geeks dedicated to publishing great graphic novels for all ages. I'm Jim Salicrup, Editor-in-Chief and part-time Comics Publishing Professor, here to reveal a few comicbook basics...

As a long-time comics editor, I've met many intelligent people who've told me that they don't understand comics. That they can't figure out how to read them. Well, today's their lucky day, as the ol' Professor intends to explain it all for you, right here, right now...

First, like most books, you read THE ONLY LIVING BOY from left to right, starting at the top of each page and working your way down. On page 5 of this very graphic novel, Chapter 5 begins with a six-sided box containing four lines of text.

SOME DAYS, YOUR BAD DECISIONS WILL STARE YOU RIGHT IN THE FACE.

Word-filled boxes in comics are called "captions," and provide narration. It could just be an omniscient narrator guiding you through the story, but in this specific case Erik Farrell is telling you his story.

Page 5 is also a full-page illustration enclosed in an even bigger box. Such pages are called "splash pages," as they often try to entice you into reading the rest of the story with some sort of "splashy" visual.

Page 6 is divided into six sections. Each of those sections, containing words and pictures in a box, is called a "panel." In the first panel, there's another caption revealing Erik's thoughts, and a rounder shape containing more words. Some folks call that round shape a "speech bubble," but serious comicbook people prefer to call it a "word balloon." Don't ask me why a balloon is any more serious than a bubble–I don't know. Jutting out from the top right side of the word balloon is a little nub coming to a point. That's called a "pointer" because it points to the person saying the words within the balloon. Some people call the pointer a "tail," especially when it appears coming from the bottom half of the word balloon, as it looks like, well, a tail.

But I'm not a man, I'm a boy.

On page 7, panel 7, Erik suddenly speaks in smaller letters that are in upper and lower

case–or with capitals and small letters. This is to indicate that he's speaking softly or even whispering.

On page 12, panel 6, an outline appears around Erik's word balloon, this is to indicate Erik is speaking louder, even shouting.

WHAT ABOUT MY FEELINGS?

...AND YOU'RE TRYING TO RUIN MINE?

Here's where it gets a little confusing. This balloon with an outline around it as well, is Baalikar's distinctive word balloon. When Baalikar speaks, it's in these balloons.

Big words

without any balloon or box containing them are generally describing the sound being created by the action depicted in the artwork. To make up for the lack of sound in comics, "sound effects" were created!

ONCE WILL TEND TO EACH OF YOU IN DUE TIME.

These word balloons with a wavy outline are the distinctive word balloons for Doctor Once.

ERIK FARRELL, PLEASE REPORT TO THE LOBBY.

This word balloon with an outline composed entirely of pointy bits is sometimes called an "electric balloon," used to indicate sound coming from electrical devices such as radios and TVs. In this case the voice is coming from a Public Address system.

And that's about it! If you're able to understand the complex science fiction elements of Chapter 6, we doubt you'll have any trouble understanding these basic elements of comic-book storytelling. If you do have any questions, feel free to contact me at the addresses indicated below. So, until we meet again in THE ONLY LIVING BOY #4 "Through the Murky Deep," class dismissed!

Thanks, JIM

STAY IN TOUCH!

EMAIL: salicrup@papercutz.com
WEB: papercutz.com
TWITTER: @papercutzgn
FACEBOOK: PAPERCUTZGRAPHICNOVELS
FAN MAIL: Papercutz, 160 Broadway, Suite 700, East Wing, New York, NY 10038